George Du Maurier

Social Pictorial Satire

George Du Maurier

Social Pictorial Satire

ISBN/EAN: 9783741194191

Manufactured in Europe, USA, Canada, Australia, Japa

Cover: Foto ©Andreas Hilbeck / pixelio.de

Manufactured and distributed by brebook publishing software
(www.brebook.com)

George Du Maurier

Social Pictorial Satire

SOCIAL PICTORIAL SATIRE

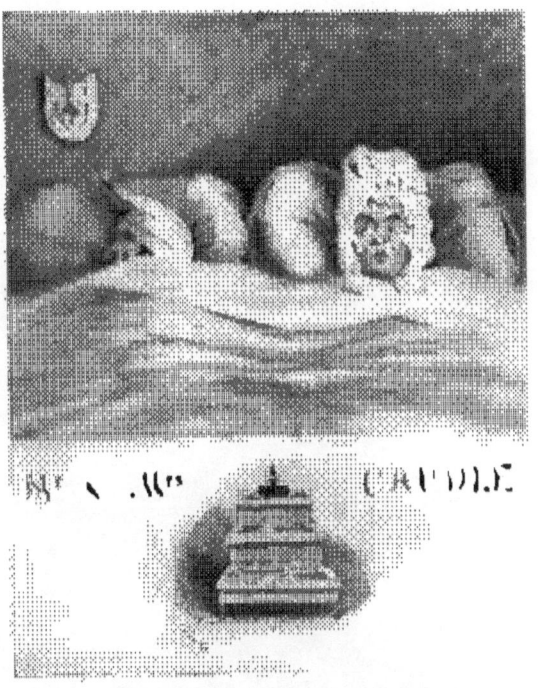

Mr. & Mrs. CAUDLE

From the original drawing by JOHN LEECH.
In the possession of JOHN KENDRICK BANGS, Esq. The lower portion has never before been reproduced.

SOCIAL PICTORIAL SATIRE. *By* GEORGE DU MAURIER, *Author of* "*Trilby*," "*The Martian*," *&c.*

WITH ILLUSTRATIONS

LONDON AND NEW YORK

HARPER & BROTHERS

ALBEMARLE ST. W.   MDCCCXCVIII

SOCIAL PICTORIAL SATIRE. *By* GEORGE DU MAURIER, *Author of* "*Trilby*," "*The Martian*," *&c.*

WITH ILLUSTRATIONS

LONDON AND NEW YORK
HARPER & BROTHERS
ALBEMARLE ST. W. MDCCCXCVIII

LIST OF ILLUSTRATIONS

LIST OF ILLUSTRATIONS

SOCIAL PICTORIAL SATIRE

IT is my purpose to speak of the craft to
which I have devoted the best years of
my life, the craft of portraying, by means
of little pen-and-ink strokes, lines, and
scratches, a small portion of the world in
which we live; such social and domestic
incidents as lend themselves to humorous or satirical treatment; the illustrated
criticism of life, of the life of our time and
country, in its lighter aspects.   · · .

The fact that I have spent so many
years in the practice of this craft does not
of itself, I am well aware, entitle me to lay
down the law about it; the mere exercise

9   ▲

of an art so patent to all, so easily under-standed of the people, does not give one any special insight into its simple mysteries, beyond a certain perception and appreciation of the technical means by which it is produced—unless one is gifted with the critical faculty, a gift apart, to the posses-sion of which I make no claim.

There are two kinds of critics of such work as ours. First there is the wide public for whom we work and by whom we are paid; "who lives to please must please to live"; and who lives by drawing for a comic periodical must manage to please the greater number. The judgment of this critic, though often sound, is not infallible; but his verdict for the time being is final, and by it we, who live by our wits and from hand to mouth, must either stand or fall.

The other critic is the expert, our fellow-craftsman, who has learned by initiation, apprenticeship, and long practice the simple secrets of our common trade. He is not quite infallible either, and is apt to concern himself more about the manner than the matter of our performance; nor is he of immediate importance, since with the public on our side we can do without him for a while, and flourish like a green bay-tree in spite of his artistic disapproval of our work; but he is not to be despised, for he is some years in advance of that other critic, the public, who may, and probably will, come round to his way of thinking in time.

The first of these two critics is typified by Molière's famous cook, who must have been a singularly honest, independent, and intelligent person, since he chose in all cases to abide by her decision, and not with an altogether unsatisfactory result to

Mankind! Such cooks are not to be found in these days—certainly not in England; but he is an unlucky craftsman who does not possess some such natural critics in his family, his home, or near it—mother, sister, friend, wife, or child—who will look over his shoulder at his little sketch, and say:

"Tommy [or Papa, or Grandpapa, as the case may be], that person you've just drawn doesn't look quite natural," or:

"That lady is not properly dressed for the person you want her to be—those hats are not worn this year," and so forth and so forth.

When you have thoroughly satisfied this household critic, then is the time to show some handy brother-craftsman your amended work, and listen gratefully when he suggests that you should put a tone on this wall, and a tree, or something, in the left middle distance to balance the composition, and raise or depress the horizon-line to get a better effect of perspective.

In speaking of some of my fellow-artists on *Punch*, and of their work, I shall try and bring both these critical methods into play—promising, however, once for all, that such criticism on my part is simply the expression of my individual taste or fancy, the taste or fancy of one who by no means pretends to the unerring acumen of Molière's cook, on the one hand, and who feels himself by no means infallible in his judgment of purely technical matters, on the other. I can only admire and say why, or why I don't; and if I fail in making you admire and disadmire with me, it will most likely be my fault as well as my misfortune.

I had originally proposed to treat of Richard Doyle, John Leech, and Charles Keene—and finally of myself, since that I should speak of myself was rather insisted upon by those who procured me the honour of speaking at all. I find, however, that there is so much to say about Leech and Keene that I have thought it better to sacrifice Richard Doyle, who belongs to a remoter period, and whose work, exquisite as it is of its kind, is so much slighter than theirs, and fills so much less of the public eye; for his connection with *Punch* did not last long. Moreover, personally I knew less of him: just enough to find that to know was to love him—a happy peculiarity he shared with his two great collaborators on *Punch*.

John Leech! What a name that was to conjure with, and is still!

I cannot find words to express what it represented to me of pure unmixed delight in my youth and boyhood, long before I ever dreamed of being an artist myself!

SOCIAL PICTORIAL SATIRE

It stands out of the path with such names as Dickens, Dumas, Byron—not indeed that I am claiming for him an equal rank with those immortals, who wielded a weapon so much more potent than a mere caricaturist's pencil! But if an artist's fame is to be measured by the mere quantity and quality of the pleasure he has given, what pinnacle is too high for John Leech!

Other men have drawn better; deeper, grander, nobler, more poetical themes have employed more accomplished pencils, even in black and white; but for making one *glad*, I can think of no one to beat him.

To be an apparently hopeless invalid at Christmas-time in some dreary, deserted, dismal little Flemish town, and to receive *Punch's Almanac* (for 1858, let us say) from some good-natured friend in England —that is a thing not to be forgotten! I

little dreamed then that I should come to
London again, and meet John Leech and
become his friend; that I should be, alas!
the last man to shake hands with him
before his death (as I believe I was), and
find myself among the officially invited
mourners by his grave; and, finally, that
I should inherit, and fill for so many years
(however indifferently), that half-page in
Punch opposite the political cartoon, and
which I had loved so well when he was
the artist!

Well, I recovered from a long and distressing ailment of my sight which had
been pronounced incurable, and came to
England, where I was introduced to
Charles Keene, with whom I quickly
became intimate, and it was he who presented me to Leech one night at one of
Mr. Arthur Lewis's smoking concerts, in
the winter of 1860. I remember feeling

somewhat nervous lest he should take me for a foreigner on account of my name, and rather unnecessarily went out of my way to assure him that I was rather more English than John Bull himself. It didn't matter in the least; I have no doubt he saw through it all: he was kindness and courtesy itself; and I experienced to the full that emotion so delightful to a young hero-worshipper in meeting face to face a world-wide celebrity whom he has long worshipped at a distance. In the words of Lord Tennyson :

" I was rapt
By all the sweet and sudden passion of youth
Towards greatness in its elder. . . ."

But it so happened at just this particular period of his artistic career and of mine that he no longer shone as a solitary star of the first magnitude in my little firmament of pictorial social satire. A new impulse had been given to the art of drawing on wood, a new school had been founded, and new methods—to draw straight from nature instead of trusting to memory and imagination—had been the artistic order of the day. Men and women, horses and dogs, landscapes and seascapes, all one can make pictures of, even chairs and tables and teacups and saucers, must be studied from the life— from the still-life, if you will—by whoever aspired to draw on wood; even angels and demons and cherubs and centaurs and mermaids must be closely imitated from. nature—or at least as much of them as could be got from the living model.

Once a Week had just appeared, and *The Cornhill Magazine.* Sir John Millais and Sir Frederick Leighton were then drawing on wood just like the ordinary mortals; Frederick Walker had just started

on his brief but splendid career; Frederick
Sandys had burst on the black-and-white
world like a meteor; and Charles Keene,
who was illustrating the *Cloister and the
Hearth* in the intervals of his *Punch* work,
had, after long and patient labour, attained
that consummate mastery of line and effect
in wood draughtsmanship that will be
for ever associated with his name ; and
his work in *Punch*, if only by virtue of
its extraordinary technical ability, made
Leech's by contrast appear slight and
almost amateurish in spite of its ease
and boldness.

So that with all my admiration for
Leech it was at the feet of Charles Keene
that I found myself sitting ; besides which
we were much together in those days,
talking endless shop, taking long walks,
riding side by side on the knife-boards
of omnibuses, dining at cheap restaurants,

making music at each other's studios.
His personal charm was great, as great
in its way as Leech's; he was democratic
and so was I, as one is bound to be when
one is impecunious and the world is one's
oyster to open with the fragile point of a
lead-pencil. His bohemian world was
mine—and I found it a very good world
and very much to my taste—a clear,
honest, wholesome, innocent, intellectual,
and most industrious British bohemia, with
lots of tobacco, lots of good music, plenty
of talk about literature and art, and not
too much victuals or drink. Many of
its denizens, that were, have become
Royal Academicians or have risen to
fame in other ways; some have had to
take a back seat in life; surprisingly few
have gone to the bad.

This world, naturally, was not Leech's;
if it had ever been, I doubt; his bohemia,

if he ever had lived in one, had been the bohemia of medicine, not of art, and he seemed to us then to be living on social heights of fame and sport and aristocratic splendour where none of us dreamed of seeking him—and he did not seek us. We hated and despised the bloated aristocracy, just as he hated and despised foreigners without knowing much about them ; and the aristocracy, to do it justice, did not pester us with its obtrusive advances.   But I never heard Leech spoken of otherwise in bohemia than with affectionate admiration, although many of us seemed to think that his best work was done.   Indeed, his work was becoming somewhat fitful in quality, and already showed occasional signs of haste and illness and fatigue ; his fun was less genial and happy, though he drew more vigorously than ever, and now and again surprised us by surpassing himself, as in his series of Briggs in the Highlands a-chasing the deer.

All that was thirty years ago and more. I may say at once that I have reconsidered the opinion I formed of John Leech at that time. Leech, it is true, is by no means the one bright particular star, but he has recovered much of his lost first magnitude: if he shines more by what he has to say than by his manner of saying it, I have come to think that that is the best thing of the two to shine by, if you cannot shine by both ; and I find that his manner was absolutely what it should have been for his purpose and his time—neither more nor less ; he had so much to say and of a kind so delightful that I have no time to pick holes in his mode of expression, which at its best has satisfied far more discriminating experts than I ;

besides which, the methods of printing
and engraving have wonderfully improved
since his day. He drew straight on the
wood block, with a lead-pencil; his
delicate grey lines had to be translated
into the uncompromising coarse black
lines of printers' ink—a ruinous process;
and what his work lost in this way is
only to be estimated by those who know.
True, his mode of expression was not
equal to Keene's—I never knew any that
was, in England, or even approached it
—but that, as Mr. Rudyard Kipling says,
is another story.

The story that I will tell now is that
of my brief acquaintance with Leech,
which began in 1860, and which I had
not many opportunities of improving till
I met him at Whitby in the autumn of
1864—a memorable autumn for me, since
I used to forgather with him every day,

and have long walks and talks with him —and dined with him once or twice at the lodgings where he was staying with his wife and son and daughter—all of whom are now dead. He was the most sympathetic, engaging, and attractive person I ever met ; not funny at all in conversation, or ever wishing to be—except now and then for a capital story, which he told in perfection.

The keynote of his character, socially, seemed to be self-effacement, high-bred courtesy, never-failing consideration for others. He was the most charming companion conceivable, having intimately known so many important and celebrated people, and liking to speak of them ; but one would never have guessed from anything he ever looked or said that he had made a whole nation, male and female, gentle and simple, old and young, laugh

as it had never laughed before or since for a quarter of a century.

He was tall, thin, and graceful, extremely handsome, of the higher Irish type; with dark hair and whiskers and complexion, and very light greyish-blue eyes; but the expression of his face was habitually sad, even when he smiled. In dress, bearing, manner, and aspect, he was the very type of the well-bred English gentleman and man of the world and good society; I never met any one to beat him in that peculiar distinction of form, which, I think, has reached its highest European development in this country. I am told the Orientals are still our superiors in deportment. But the natural man in him was still the best. Thackeray and Sir John Millais, not bad judges, and men with many friends, have both said that they personally loved John

27

Leech better than any man they ever knew.

At this time he was painting in oil, and on an enlarged scale, some of his more specially popular sketches in *Punch*, and very anxious to succeed with them, but nervously diffident of success with them, even with οἱ πολλοί. He was not at his happiest in these efforts ; and there was something pathetic in his earnest-ness and perseverance in attempting a thing so many can do, but which he could not do for want of a better train-ing ; while he could do the inimitable so easily.

I came back to town before Leech, and did not see him again until the following October. On Saturday afternoon, the 28th, I called at his house, No. 6 The Terrace, Kensington, with a very elaborate drawing in pencil by myself, which I presented to him as a souvenir, and with which he seemed much pleased.

He was already working at the *Punch Almanac* for '65, at a window on the second floor overlooking the street. (I have often gazed up at it since.) He seemed very ill, so sad and depressed that I could scarcely speak to him for sheer sympathy; I felt he would never get through the labour of that almanac, and left him with the most melancholy forebodings.

Monday morning the papers announced his death on Sunday, October 29th, from angina pectoris, the very morning after I had seen him.

I was invited by Messrs. Bradbury and Evans, the publishers of *Punch*, to the funeral, which took place at Kensal Green. It was the most touching sight imaginable. The grave was near Thackeray's, who had died the year before. There were crowds of people, Charles Dickens among them ; Canon Hole, a great friend of Leech's, and who has written most affectionately about him, read the service ; and when the coffin was lowered into the grave, John Millais burst into tears and loud sobs, setting an example that was followed all round ; we all forgot our manhood and cried like women ! I can recall no funeral in my time where simple grief and affection have been so openly and spontaneously displayed by so many strangers as well as friends—not even in France, where people are more demonstrative than here. No burial in Westminster Abbey that I have ever seen ever gave such an impression of universal honour, love, and regret.

"Whom the gods love die young." He was only forty-six !

I was then invited to join the *Punch* staff and take Leech's empty chair at the weekly dinner—and bidden to cut my initials on the table, by his ; his monogram as it was carved by him is J. L. under a leech in a bottle, dated 1854 ; and close by on the same board are the initials W. M. T.

I flatter myself that convivially, at least, my small D. M., carved in impenetrable oak, will go down to posterity in rather distinguished company !

If ever there was a square English hole, and a square English peg to fit it, that hole was *Punch*, and that peg was John Leech. He was John Bull himself, but John Bull refined and civilised—John Bull polite, modest, gentle—full of self-respect and self-restraint, and with all the bully softened out of him ; manly first and gentlemanly after, but very soon after; more at home perhaps in the club, the drawing-room, and the hunting-field, in Piccadilly and the Park, than in the farm or shop or market-place; a normal Englishman of the upper middle class, with but one thing abnormal about him, viz., his genius, which was of the kind to give the greater pleasure to the greater number—and yet delight the most fastidious of his day—and I think of ours. One must be very ultra-æsthetic, even now, not to feel his charm.

He was all of a piece, and moved and worked with absolute ease, freedom, and certainty, within the limits nature had assigned him—and his field was a very large one. He saw and represented the whole panorama of life that came within his immediate ken with an unwavering consistency, from first to last; from a broadly humorous, though mostly sym-

pathetic point ·of view that never changed
—a very delightful point of view, if not
the highest conceivable.

Hand and eye worked with brain in
singular harmony, and all three improved
together contemporaneously, with a paral-
lelism most interesting to note, as one
goes through the long series of his social
pictures from the beginning.

He has no doubts or hesitations—no
bewildering subtleties—no seeking from
twelve to fourteen o'clock—either in his
ideas or technique, which very soon becomes an excellent technique, thoroughly
suited to his ideas—rapid, bold, spirited,
full of colour, breadth, and movement—
troubling itself little about details that will
not help the telling of his story—for before
everything else he has his story to tell,
and it must either make you laugh or
lightly charm you—and he tells it in the

quickest, simplest, down-rightest pencil
strokes, although it is often a complicated
story !

For there are not only the funny people
and the pretty people acting out their
little drama in the foreground—there is
the scene in which they act, and the
middle distance, and the background
beyond, and the sky itself; beautiful
rough landscapes and seascapes and sky-
scapes, winds and weathers, boisterous or
sunny seas, rain and storm and cloud—all
the poetry of nature, that he feels most
acutely while his little people are being so
unconsciously droll in the midst of it all.
He is a king of impressionists, and his
impression becomes ours on the spot—
never to be forgotten! It is all so quick
and fresh and strong, so simple, pat, and
complete, so direct from mother Nature
herself! It has about it the quality of

inevitableness—those are the very people who would have acted and spoken in just that manner, and we meet them every day —the expression of the face, the movement and gesture, in anger, terror, dismay, scorn, conceit, tenderness, elation, triumph. . . . Whatever the mood, they could not have looked or acted otherwise —it is life itself. An optimistic life in which joyousness prevails, and the very woes and discomfitures are broadly comical to us who look on—like some one who has sea-sickness, or a headache after a Greenwich banquet—which are about the most tragic things he has dealt with.

(I am speaking of his purely social sketches. For in his admirable large cuts, political and otherwise serious, his satire is often bitter and biting indeed ; and his tragedy almost Hogarthian.)

Like many true humorists, he was of a

melancholy temperament, and no doubt felt attracted by all that was mirthful and bright, and in happy contrast to his habitual mood. Seldom if ever does a drop of his inner sadness ooze out through his pencil-point—and never a drop of gall ; and I do not remember one cynical touch in his whole series.

In his tastes and habits he was by nature aristocratic; he liked the society of those who were well dressed, well bred and refined like himself, and perhaps a trifle conventional; he conformed quite spontaneously and without effort to upper-class British ideal of his time, and had its likes and dislikes. But his strongest predilections of all are common to the British race : his love of home, his love of sport, his love of the horse and the hound —especially his love of the pretty woman —the pretty woman of the normal, whole-

some English type. This charming creature so dear to us all pervades his show
from beginning to end—she is a creation
of his, and he thoroughly loves her, and
draws her again and again with a fondness
that is half lover-like and half paternal—
her buxom figure, her merry bright eyes
and fresh complexion and flowing ringlets,
and pursed-up lips like Cupid's bow. Nor
is he ever tired of displaying her feet and
ankles (and a little more) in gales of wind
on cliff and pier and parade, or climbing
the Malvern Hills. When she puts on
goloshes it nearly breaks his heart, and
he would fly to other climes! He revels
in her infantile pouts and jealousies and
heart-burnings and butterfly delights and
lisping mischiefs; her mild, innocent flir-
tations with beautiful young swells, whose
cares are equally light.

She is a darling, and he constantly calls

her so to her face. Her favourite seaside nook becomes the mermaid's haunt; her back hair flies and dries in the wind, and disturbs the peace of the too susceptible Punch. She is a little amazon *pour rire*, and rides across country, and drives (even a hansom sometimes, with a pair of magnificent young whiskerandoes smoking their costly cigars inside); she is a toxophilite, and her arrow sticks, for it is barbed with innocent seduction, and her bull's-eye is the soft military heart. She wears a cricket-cap and breaks Aunt Sally's nose seven times; she puts her pretty little foot upon the croquet-ball— and croquet'd you are completely! With what glee she would have rinked and tennised if he had lived a little longer!

She is light of heart, and perhaps a little of head! Her worst trouble is when the captain gives the wing of the fowl to

"IN THE BAY OF BISCAY O."

The Last Sweet Thing in Hats and Walking-Sticks.—*Punch*, September 27, 1862.

some other darling who might be her twin-sister; her most terrible nightmare is when she dreams that great stupid Captain Sprawler upsets a dish of trifle 'over her new lace dress with the blue satin slip; but next morning she is herself again, and rides in the Row, and stops to speak with that great stupid Captain Sprawler, who is very nice to look at, whose back is very beautiful, and who sprawls most gracefully over the railings, and pays her those delightful, absurd compliments about her and her horse "being such a capital pair," while, as a foil to so much grace and splendour, a poor little snub-nosed, ill-dressed, ill-conditioned dwarf of a snob looks on, sucking the top of his cheap cane in abject admiration and hopeless envy! Then she pats and kisses the nice soft nose of Cornet Flinders's hunter, which is "deucedly aggravating for

Cornet Flinders, you know "—but when that noble sportsman is frozen out and cannot hunt, she plays scratch-cradle with him in the boudoir of her father's country house, or pitches chocolate into his mouth · from the oak landing; and she lets him fasten the skates on to her pretty feet. Happy cornet! And she plays billiards with her handsome cousin—a guardsman at least—and informs him that she is just eighteen to his love—and stands under the mistletoe and asks this enviable relation of hers to show her what the garroter's hug is like; and when he proceeds to do so she calls out in distress because his pointed waxed moustache has scratched her pretty cheek; and when Mr. Punch is there, at dinner, she and a sister darling pull crackers across his august white waistcoat, and scream in pretty terror at the explosion; to that worthy's excessive jubilation, for Mr. Punch is Leech himself, and nothing she does can ever be amiss in his eyes!

Sometimes, indeed, she is seriously transfixed herself, and bids Mr. Tongs, the hairdresser, cut off a long lock of her hair where it will not be missed—and she looks so lovely under the smart of Cupid's arrow that we are frantically jealous of the irresistible warrior for whom the jetty tress is destined. In short, she is innocence and liveliness and health incarnate—a human kitten.

When she marries the gilded youth with the ambrosial whiskers, their honey-mooning is like playing at being married, their heartless billings and cooings are enchanting to see. She will have no troubles—Leech will take good care of that; her matrimonial tiffs will be of the slightest; hers will be a well-regulated household ; the course of her conjugal love will run smooth in spite of her little indiscretions—for, like Bluebeard's wife, she can be curious at times, and coax and wheedle to know the mysteries of Freemasonry, and cry because Edwin will not reveal the secret of Mr. Percy, the horse-tamer ; and how Edwin can resist such an appeal is more than we can understand! But soon they will have a large family, . and live happy ever after, and by the time their eldest-born is thirteen years old, the darling of fourteen years back will be a regular materfamilias, stout, matronly, and rather severe ; and Edwin will be fat, bald, and middle-aged, and bring home a bundle of asparagus and a nice new perambulator to celebrate the wedding-day !

And he loves her brothers and cousins, military or otherwise, just as dearly, and makes them equally beautiful to the eye, with those lovely drooping whiskers that used to fall and brush their bosoms, their smartly waistcoated bosoms, a quarter of a century ago! He dresses them even better than the darlings, and has none but the kindliest and gentlest satire for their little vanities and conceits—for they have no real vices, these charming youths, beyond smoking too much and betting a little and getting gracefully tipsy at race-meetings and Greenwich dinners—and sometimes running into debt with their tailors, I suppose! And then how boldly they ride to hounds, and how splendidly they fight in the Crimea! how lightly they dance at home! How healthy, good-humoured, and manly they are, with all their vagaries of dress and jewellery and accent! It is easy to forgive them if they give the whole of their minds to their white neckties, or are dejected because

they have lost the little gridiron off their
chatelaine, or lose all presence of mind
when a smut settles on their noses, and
turn faint at the sight of Mrs. Gamp's
umbrella!

And next to these enviable beings he
loves and reveres the sportsman. One is
made to feel that the true sportsman,
whether he shoots or hunts or fishes, is an
august being, as he ought to be in Great
Britain, and Leech has done him full justice with his pencil. He is no subject for
flippant satire ; so there he sits his horse,
or stalks through his turnip-field, or handles
his rod like a god! Handsome, well-
appointed from top to toe, aristocratic to
the finger-tips—a most impressive figure,
the despair of foreigners, the envy of all
outsiders at home (including the present
lecturer)!

He has never been painted like this

A SPECIMEN OF PLUCK.

RUGGLES. "Hold hard, Master George It's too wide, and uncommon deep."
MASTER GEORGE. "All right, Ruggles! We can both swim!"—*Punch*

before ! What splendid lords and squires, fat or lean, hook-nosed or eagle-eyed, well tanned by sun and wind, in faultless kit, on priceless mounts ! How redolent they are of health and wealth, and the secure consciousness of high social position—of the cool business-like self-importance that sits so well on those who are knowing in the noblest pursuit that can ever employ the energies and engross the mind of a well-born Briton ; for they can ride almost as well as their grooms, these mighty hunters before the Lord, and know the country almost as well as the huntsman himself! And what sons and grandsons and granddaughters are growing up round them, on delightful ponies no gate, hedge, or brook can dismay—nothing but the hard high-road!

It is a glorious, exhilarating scene, with the beautiful wintry landscape stretching

away to the cloudy November sky, and
the lords and ladies gay, and the hounds,
and the frosty-faced, short-tempered old
huntsman, the very perfection of his kind ;
and the poor cockney snobs on their hired
screws, and the meek clod-hopping labourers looking on excited and bewil-
dered, happy for a moment at beholding
so much happiness in their betters.

To have seen these sketches of the
hunting-field is to have been there in
person. It is almost the only hunting
that I ever had—and probably ever shall
have—and I am almost content that it
should be so! It is so much easier
and simpler to draw for *Punch* than to
drive across country! And then, as a
set-off to all this successful achievement,
this pride and pomp and circumstance
of glorious sport, we have the immortal
and ever-beloved figure of Mr. Briggs,

ONE OF MR. BRIGGS'S ADVENTURES IN THE HIGHLANDS

After aiming for a Quarter of an Hour Mr. B. fires both of his Barrels—and—misses!!!!

Tableau—The Forester's Anguish.—*Punch*, 186-.

whom I look upon as Leech's master-piece—the example above all others of the most humorous and good-natured satire that was ever penned or pencilled. The more ridiculous he is the more we love him; he is more winning and sympathetic than even Mr. Pickwick himself, and I almost think a greater creation! Besides, it took two to make Mr. Pickwick, the author and the artist, whereas Mr. Briggs issued fully equipped from the brain of Leech alone!

Not indeed that all unauthorised gallopers after the fox find forgiveness in the eyes of Leech. Woe to the vulgar little cockney snob who dares to obtrude his ugly mug and his big cigar and his hired, broken-winded rip on these hallowed and thrice - happy hunting - grounds! — an earthenware pot among vessels of brass; the punishment shall be made to fit the crime; better if he fell off and his horse rolled over him than that he should dress and ride and look like that! For the pain of broken bones is easier to bear than the scorn of a true British sportsman!

Then there are the fishermen who never catch any fish, but whom no stress of weather can daunt or distress. There they sit or stand with the wind blowing or the rain soaking, in dark landscapes with ruffled streams and ominous clouds, and swaying trees that turn up the whites of their leaves—one almost hears the wind rush through them. One almost forgets the comical little forlorn figure who gives such point to all the angry turbulence of nature in the impression produced by the *mise en scène* itself—an impression so happily, so vividly suggested by a few rapid, instructive pencil strokes and thumb

THANK GOODNESS! FLY-FISHING HAS BEGUN!

MILLER. "Don't they really, perhaps they'll bite better towards the cool of the evening, they mostly do."
—*Punch*, 1857.

smudges that it haunts the memory like a dream.

He loves such open-air scenes so sincerely, he knows so well how to express and communicate the perennial charm they have for him, that the veriest bookworm becomes a sportsman through sheer sympathy—by the mere fact of looking at them.

And how many people and things he loves that most of us love!—it would take all night to enumerate them—the good authoritative pater-, and materfamilias ; the delightful little girls ; the charming cheeky school-boys ; the jolly little street Arabs, who fill old gentlemen's letter-boxes with oyster-shells and gooseberry-skins ; the cabmen, the busmen ; the policemen with the old-fashioned chimney-pot hat ; the old bathing-women, and Jack-ashores, and jolly old tars — his

British tar is irresistible, whether he is hooking a sixty-four pounder out of the Black Sea, or riding a Turk, or drinking tea instead of grog and complaining of its strength! There seems to be hardly a mirthful corner of English life that Leech has not seen and loved and painted in this singularly genial and optimistic manner.

His loves are many and his hates are few—but he is a good hater all the same. He hates Mawworm and Stiggins, and so do we. He hates the foreigner—whom he does not know, as heartily as Thackeray does, who seems to know him so well—with a hatred that seems to me a little unjust, perhaps : all France is not in Leicester Square ; many Frenchmen can dress and ride, drive and shoot as well as anybody ; and they began to use the tub very soon after we did—a dozen

"Oh, crikee hin 'Tommy! s'ppose we stay at
'ole thy footman I au't diggercut 'it is
la des in the carridges!"

" THE JOLLY LITTLE STREET ARABS "

From the original drawing for *Punch* in possession of John Kendrick Bangs, Esq.

years or so, perhaps—say after the *coup d'état* in 1851.

Then he hates with a deadly hatred all who make music in the street or next door —and preach in the crossways and bawl their wares on the parade. What would he have said of the Salvation Army? He is haunted by the bark of his neighbour's dog, by the crow of his neighbour's Cochin China cock; he cannot even bear his neighbour to have his chimney swept; and as for the Christmas waits—we all remember *that* tragic picture! This exaggerated aversion to noises became a disease with him, and possibly hastened his end.

Among his pet hates we must not forget the gorgeous flunky and the guzzling alderman, the leering old fop, the rascally book-maker, the sweating Jew tradesman, and the poor little snob (the 'Arry of his day) who tries vainly to grow a moustache, and wears such a shocking bad hat, and iron heels to his shoes, and shuns the Park during the riots for fear of being pelted for a "haristocrat," and whose punishment I think is almost in excess of his misdemeanor.   To succeed in over-dressing one's self (as his swells did occasionally without marring their beauty) is almost as ignominious as to fail ; and when the failure comes from want of means, there is also almost a pathetic side to it.

And he is a little bit hard on old frumps, with fat ankles and scraggy bosoms and red noses—but anyhow we are made to laugh—*quod erat demonstrandum.* We also know that he has a strong objection to cold mutton for dinner, and much prefers a whitebait banquet at Greenwich, or a nice well-

DOING A LITTLE BUSINESS

OLD EQUESTRIAN. "Well, but—you're not the boy I left my horse with."

BOY. "No, sir: I last speklliated, and bought 'im of t'other boy for a bargen y'."—*Punch.*

ordered repast at the Star and Garter. So do we.

And the only thing he feared is the horse. Nimrod as he is, and the happiest illustrator of the hunting-field that ever was, he seems for ever haunted by a terror of the heels of that noble animal he drew so well—and I thoroughly sympathise with him !

In all the series the chief note is joyousness, high spirits, the pleasure of being alive. There is no *Weltschmerz* in his happy world, where all is for the best— no hankering after the moon, no discontent with the present order of things. Only one little lady discovers that the world is hollow, and her doll is stuffed with bran ; only one gorgeous swell has exhausted the possibilities of this life, and finds out that he is at loss for a new sensation. So what does he do ? Cut his throat? Go and shoot big game in Africa? No; he visits the top of the Monument on a rainy day, or invites his brother-swells to a Punch and Judy show in his rooms, or rides to White-chapel and back on an omnibus with a bag of periwinkles, and picks them out with a pin!

Even when his humour is at its broadest, and he revels in almost panto-mimic fun, he never loses sight of truth and nature — never strikes a false or uncertain note. Robinson goes to an evening party with a spiked knuckle-duster in his pocket and sits down. Jones digs an elderly party called Smith in the back with the point of his umbrella, under the impression that it is his friend Brown. A charming little street Arab prints the soles of his muddy feet on a smart old gentleman's white evening waistcoat.

Tompkyns writes Henrietta on the sands under two hearts transfixed by an arrow, and his wife, whose name is Matilda, catches him in the act. An old gentleman, maddened by a bluebottle, smashes all his furniture and breaks every window-pane but one—where the bluebottle is. And in all these scenes one does not know which is the most irresistible, the most inimitable — the mere drollery or the dramatic truth of gesture and facial expression.

The way in which every-day people really behave in absurd situations and under comically trying circumstances is quite funny enough for him; and if he exaggerates a little and goes beyond the absolute prose of life in the direction of caricature, he never deviates a hair's-breadth from the groove human nature has laid down. There is exaggeration, but no distortion. The most wildly funny people are low comedians of the highest order, whose fun is never forced and never fails; they found themselves on fact, and only burlesque what they have seen in actual life—they never evolve their fun from the depths of their inner consciousness; and in this naturalness, for me, lies the greatness of Leech. There is nearly always a tenderness in the laughter he excites, born of the touch of nature that makes the whole world kin !

Where most of all he gives us a sense of the exuberant joyousness and buoyancy of life is in the sketches of the seaside— the newly discovered joys of which had then not become commonplace to people of the middle class. The good old sea- side has grown rather stale by this time— the very children of to-day dig and paddle

A TOLERABLY BROAD HINT

"Oh, I beg your pardon, sir, but you didn't say as we were to pull up anywhere, did you, sir?"

—*Punch*, 1859.

in a half-perfunctory sort of fashion, with a certain stolidity, and are in strange contrast to those highly elate and enchanting little romps that fill his seaside pictures.

Indeed, nothing seems so jolly, nothing seems so funny, now, as when Leech was drawing for *Punch.* The gaiety of one nation at least has been eclipsed by his death. Is it merely that there is no such light humorist to see and draw for us in a frolicsome spirit all the fun and the jollity? Is it because some of us have grown old? Or is it that the British people themselves have changed and gone back to their old way of taking their pleasure sadly?

Everything is so different, somehow; the very girls themselves have grown a head taller, and look serious, stately, and dignified, like Olympian goddesses, even when they are dancing and playing lawn-tennis.

I for one should no more dream of calling them the darlings than I should dare to kiss them under the mistletoe, were I ever so splendid a young captain. Indeed I am too prostrate in admiration—I can only suck the top of my stick and gaze in jealous ecstasy, like one of Leech's little snobs.   They are no longer pretty as their grandmothers were—whom Leech drew so well in the old days! They are *beautiful!*

And then they are so cultivated, and *know* such a lot—of books, of art, of science, of politics, and theology—of the world, the flesh, and the devil. They actually think for themselves; they have broken loose and jumped over the ring-fence; they have taken to the water, these lovely chicks, and swim like ducklings, to

the dismay of those good old cocks and
hens, their grandparents! And my love
of them is tinged with awe, as was Leech's
love of that mighty, beautiful, but most
uncertain quadruped, the thoroughbred
horse—for, like him, when they are good,
they are very, very good, but when they
are bad, they are horrid. We have
changed other things as well : the swell
has become the masher, and is a terrible
dull dog ; the poor little snob has blos-
somed into a blatant 'Arry, and no longer
wears impossible hats and iron heels to his
boots ; he has risen in the social scale, and
holds his own without fear or favour in
the Park and everywhere else. To be
taken for a haristocrat is his dream !—
even if he be pelted for it. In his higher
developments he becomes a " bounder,"
and bounds away in most respectable
West End ball-rooms. He is the only

person with any high spirits left—perhaps that is why high spirits have gone out of fashion, like boxing the watch and wrenching off door-knockers!

And the snob of our day is quite a different person, more likely than not to be found hobnobbing with dukes and duchesses—as irreproachable in dress and demeanour as Leech himself. Thackeray discovered and christened him for us long ago ; and he is related to most of us, and moves in the best society. He has even ceased to brag of his intimacy with the great, they have become so commonplace to him ; and if he swaggers at all, it is about his acquaintance with some popular actor or comic vocalist whom he is privileged to call by his christian-name.

And those splendid old grandees of high rank, so imposing of aspect, so crushing to us poor mortals by mere virtue not of their wealth and title alone, but of their high-bred distinction of feature and bearing — to which Leech did such ample justice—what has become of them?

They are like the snows of yester-year! They have gone the way of their beautiful chariots with the elaborate armorial bearings and the tasselled hammercloth, the bewigged, cocked-hatted coachman, and the two gorgeous flunkies hanging on behind. Sir Gorgeous Midas has beaten the dukes in mere gorgeousness, flunkies and all—burlesqued the vulgar side of them, and unconsciously shamed it out of existence ; made swagger and ostentation unpopular by his own evil example— actually improved the manners of the great by sheer mimicry of their defects. He has married his sons and his daughters to them and spoiled the noble curve of those lovely noses that Leech drew so well, and brought them down a peg in many ways, and given them a new lease of life ; and he has enabled us to discover that they are not of such different clay from ourselves after all. All the old slavish formulæ of deference and respect— "Your Grace," "Your Ladyship," "My Lord"—that used to run so glibly off our tongues whenever we had a chance, are now left to servants and shopkeepers ; and my slight experience of them, for one, is that they do not want to be toadied a bit, and that they are very polite, well-bred, and most agreeable people.

If we may judge of our modern aristocracy by that very slender fragment of our contemporary fiction, mostly American, that still thinks it worth writing about, our young noble of to-day is the most good-humoured, tolerant, simple-hearted, simple-minded, unsophisticated creature alive—

thinking nothing of his honours—prostrate under the little foot of some fair Yankee, who is just as likely as not to jilt him for some transatlantic painter not yet known to fame.

Compare this unpretending youth to one of Bulwer's heroes, or Disraeli's, or even Thackeray's! And his simple old duke of a father and his dowdy old duchess of a mother are almost as devoid of swagger as himself; they seem to apologise for their very existence, if we may trust these American chroniclers who seem to know them so well; and I really think we no longer care to hear and read about them quite so much as we did—unless it be in the society papers!

But all these past manners and customs that some of us can remember so well—all these obsolete people, from the heavily whiskered swell to the policeman with the leather-bound chimney-pot hat, from good pater- and mater-familias who were actually looked up to and obeyed by their children, to the croquet-playing darlings in the pork-pie hats and huge crinolines—all survive and will survive for many a year in John Leech's "Pictures of Life and Character."

Except for a certain gentleness, kindliness, and self-effacing modesty common to both, and which made them appear almost angelic in the eyes of many who knew them, it would be difficult to imagine a greater contrast to Leech than Charles Keene.

Charles Keene was absolutely unconventional, and even almost eccentric. He dressed more with a view to artistic picturesqueness than to fashion, and despised gloves and chimney-pot hats, and black coats and broadcloth generally.

From a photograph by Elliott and Fry, London.

CHARLES KEENE

Scotch tweed was good enough for him in town and country alike. Though a Tory in politics, he was democratic in his tastes and habits. He liked to smoke his short black pipe on the tops of omnibuses; he liked to lay and light his own fire and cook his mutton-chop upon it. He had a passion for music and a beautiful voice, and sang with a singular pathos and charm, but he preferred the sound of his bagpipes to that of his own singing, and thought that you must prefer it too!

He was for ever sketching in pen and ink, indoors and out—he used at one time to carry a little ink-bottle at his button-hole, and steel pens in his waistcoat-pocket, and thus equipped he would sketch whatever took his fancy in his walks abroad — houses, 'busses, cabs, people—bits of street and square, scaffold-

ings, hoardings with advertisements—sea,
river, moor, lake, and mountain—what has
he not sketched with that masterly pen
that had already been so carefully trained
by long and arduous practice in a life-
school ? His heart was in his work from
first to last ; beyond his bagpipes and his
old books (for he was a passionate reader),
he seemed to have no other hobby. His
facility in sketching became phenomenal,
as also his knowledge of what to put in
and what to leave out, so that the effect
he aimed at should be secured in perfection and with the smallest appearance
of labour.

Among his other gifts he had a physical
gift of inestimable value for such work as
ours—namely, a splendid hand—a large,
muscular, well-shaped, and most workman-
like hand, whose long deft fingers could
move with equal ease and certainty in all

directions. I have seen it at work—and it was a pleasure to watch its acrobatic dexterity, its unerring precision of touch. It could draw with nonchalant facility parallel straight lines, or curved, of just the right thickness and distance from each other—almost as regular as if they had been drawn with ruler or compass— almost, but not *quite*. The quiteness would have made them mechanical, and robbed them of their charm of human handicraft. A cunning and obedient slave, this wonderful hand, for which no command from the head could come amiss — a slave, moreover, that had most thoroughly learned its business by long apprenticeship to one especial trade, like the head and like the eye that guided it.

Leech, no doubt, had a good natural hand, that swept about with enviable freedom and boldness, but for want of early discipline it could not execute these miracles of skill; and the commands that came from the head also lacked the preciseness which results from patiently acquired and well-digested knowledge, so that Mr. Hand was apt now and then to zigzag a little on its own account — in backgrounds, on floors and walls, under chairs and tables, whenever a little tone was felt to be desirable — sometimes in the shading of coats and trousers and ladies' dresses.

But it never took a liberty with a human face or a horse's head; and whenever it went a little astray you could always read between the lines and know exactly what it meant.

There is no difficulty in reading between Keene's lines; every one of them has its unmistakable definite intimation;

every one is the right line in the right place!

We must remember that there are no such things as lines in nature. Whether we use them to represent a human profile, the depth of a shadow, the darkness of a cloak or a thunder-cloud, they are mere conventional symbols. They were invented a long time ago, by a distinguished sportsman who was also a heaven-born amateur artist — the John Leech of his day—who engraved for us (from life) the picture of mammoth on one of its own tusks.

And we have accepted them ever since as the cheapest and simplest way of interpreting in black and white for the wood-engraver the shapes and shadows and colours of nature. They may be scratchy, feeble, and uncertain, or firm and bold—thick and thin—straight, curved,

parallel, or irregular—cross-hatched once,
twice, a dozen times, at any angle—every
artist has his own way of getting his effect.
But some ways are better than others, and
I think Keene's is the firmest, loosest,
simplest, and best way that ever was, and
—the most difficult to imitate. His mere
pen-strokes have, for the expert, a beauty
and an interest quite apart from the thing
they are made to depict, whether he uses
them as mere outlines to express the shape
of things animate or inanimate, even such
shapeless, irregular things as the stones on
a sea-beach—or in combination to suggest
the tone and colour of a dress-coat, or
a drunkard's nose, of a cab or omnibus
—of a distant mountain with miles of
atmosphere between it and the figures in
the foreground.

His lines are as few as can be—he is
most economical in this respect and loves

THE SNOWSTORM, JAN. 2, 1867

CABBY (*petulantly—the Cabbies seem to have lost their tempers*). "It's no use your a-calling o' me, Sir! Got such a Job with these 'ere Two as I'll last me a Fortnight!"

—*Punch*, January 19, 1867.

to leave as much white paper as he can ;
but one feels in his best work that one line
more or one line less would impair the
perfection of the whole—that of all the
many directions, curves, and thicknesses
they might have taken he has inevitably
hit upon just the right one. He has
beaten all previous records in this respect
—in this country, at least. I heard a
celebrated French painter say : " He is
a great man, your Charles Keene ; he take
a pen and ink and a bit of paper, and wiz
a half-dozen strokes he know 'ow to frame
a gust of wind ! " I think myself that
Leech could frame a gust of wind as
effectually as Keene, by the sheer force
of his untaught natural instinct—of his
genius ; but not with the deftness—this
economy of material—this certainty of
execution—this consummate knowledge
of effect.

To borrow a simile from music, there are certain tunes so fresh and sweet and pretty that they please at once and for ever, like " Home, Sweet Home," or " The Last Rose of Summer "; they go straight to the heart of the multitude, however slight the accompaniment—a few simple chords—they hardly want an accompaniment at all.

Leech's art seems to me of just such a happy kind ; he draws—I mean he scores like an amateur who has not made a very profound study of harmony, and sings his pretty song to his simple accompaniment with so sweet and true a natural voice that we are charmed. It is the magic of nature, whereas Keene is a very Sebastian Bach in his counterpoint. There is nothing of the amateur about him ; his knowledge of harmony in black and white is complete and thorough ; mere consummate scoring has become to him a second nature ; each separate note of his voice reveals the long training of the professional singer ; and if his tunes are less obviously sweet and his voice less naturally winning and sympathetic than Leech's, his æsthetic achievement is all the greater. It is to his brother-artists rather than to the public at large that his most successful appeal is made—but with an intensity that can only be gained by those who have tried in vain to do what he has done, and who thereby know how difficult it is. His real magic is that of art.

This perhaps accounts for the unmistakable fact that Leech's popularity has been so much greater than Keene's, and I believe is still. Leech's little melodies of the pencil (to continue the parallel with the sister art) are like Volkslieder—

national airs—and more directly reach
the national heart. Transplant them to
other lands that have pencil Volkslieder
of their own (though none, I think, com-
parable to his for fun and sweetness and
simplicity) and they fail to please as much,
while their mere artistic qualities are not
such as to find favour among foreign
experts, whereas Keene actually gains by
such a process. He is as much admired
by the artists of France and Germany
as by our own—if not more. For some
of his shortcomings—such as his lack of
feeling for English female beauty, his
want of perception, perhaps his disdain,
of certain little eternal traits and con-
ventions and differences that stamp the
various grades of our social hierarchy—do
not strike them, and nothing interferes
with their complete appreciation of his
craftsmanship.

WAITING FOR THE LANDLORD!

RUNNAWAY (*getting impatient*). "Bedad, they ought to be here be this toime! Sure, Thinor, I hope the ould gintleman hasn't mit wid an accident::!"—(*Punch*, July 27, 1893)

Perhaps, also, Leech's frequent verification of our manly British pluck and honesty, and proficiency in sport, and wholesomeness and cleanliness of body and mind, our general physical beauty and distinction, and his patriotic tendency to contrast our exclusive possession of these delightful gifts with the deplorable absence of them in any country but our own, may fail to enlist the sympathies of the benighted foreigner.

Whereas there is not much to humiliate the most touchy French or German reader of *Punch*, or excite his envy, in Charles Keene's portraiture of our race. He is impartial and detached, and the most rabid Anglophobe may frankly admire him without losing his self-esteem. The English lower middle class and people, that Keene has depicted with such judicial freedom from either prejudice or prepossession, have many virtues; but they are not especially conspicuous for much vivacity or charm of aspect or gainliness of demeanour; and he has not gone out of his way to idealise them.

Also, he seldom if ever gibes at those who have not been able to resist the temptations (as Mr. Gilbert would say) of belonging to other nations.

Thus in absolute craftsmanship and technical skill, in the ease and beauty of his line, his knowledge of effect, his complete mastery over the material means at his disposal, Charles Keene seems to me as superior to Leech as Leech is to him in grace, in human naturalness and geniality of humour, in accurate observation of life, in keenness of social perception, and especially in width of range.

The little actors on Leech's stage are nearly all of them every-day people—

A STROKE OF BUSINESS

VILLAGE HAIRDRESSER ("*who with dauntless breast" has undertaken for instance to lop off the other boy*). "If any of yer wants to see what we're a Paintin' of it's a 'Apenny a 'Ead, but you mustn't make no Remarks."—*Punch*, May 4, 1867.

types one is constantly meeting. High or low, tipsy or sober, vulgar or refined, pleasant or the reverse, we knew them all before Leech ever drew them; and our recognition of them on his page is full of delight at meeting old familiar friends and seeing them made fun of for our amusement.

Whereas a great many of Keene's middle-class protagonists are peculiar and exceptional, and much of their humour lies in their eccentricity, they are characters themselves, rather than types of English characters. Are they really observed and drawn from life, do they really exist just as they are, or are they partly evolved from the depths of an inner consciousness that is not quite satisfied with life just as it is?

They are often comic, with their exquisitely drawn faces so full of subtlety

—intensely comic! Their enormous per-
plexities about nothing, their utter guile-
lessness, their innocence of the wicked
world and its ways, make them engaging
sometimes in spite of a certain ungainliness
of gesture, dress, and general behaviour
that belongs to them, and which delighted
Charles Keene, who was the reverse of
ungainly, just as the oft-recurring tipsi-
ness of his old gentlemen delighted him,
though he was the most abstemious of
men. I am now speaking of his middle-
class people—those wonderful philistines
of either sex; those elaborately capped
and corpulent old ladies; those mutton-
chop-whiskered, middle-aged gentlemen
with long upper lips and florid com-
plexions, receding chins, noses almost
horizontal in their prominence; those
artless damsels who trouble themselves
so little about the latest fashions; those

"NONE O' YOUR LARKS"

GIGANTIC NAVVY. "Let's walk between yer, Gents; folks 'll think you've took
up a Deserter."—*Punch*, October 19, 1861.

feeble-minded, hirsute swells with the sloping shoulders and the broad hips and the little hats cocked on one side; those unkempt, unspoiled, unspotted from the world brothers of the brush, who take in their own milk, and so complacently ignore all the rotten conventionalism of our over-civilised existence.

When he takes his subjects from the classes beneath these, he is, if not quite so funny, at his best, I think. His costermongers and policemen, his omnibus drivers and conductors and cabbies, are inimitable studies; and as for his 'busses and cabs, I really cannot find words to express my admiration of them. In these, as in his street scenes and landscapes, he is unapproached and unapproachable.

Nor must we forget his canny Scotsmen, his Irish labourers and peasants, his

splendid English navvies, and least of all
his volunteers—he and Leech might be
called the pillars of the Volunteer movement, from the manner, so true, so sympathetic, and so humorous, in which they
have immortalised its beginning.

Charles Keene is seldom a satirist.
His nature was too tolerant and too sweet
for hate, and that makes him a bad and
somewhat perfunctory hater. He tries to
hate 'Arry, but he can't, for he draws an
ideal 'Arry that surely never was, and
thus his shaft misses the mark : compare
his 'Arry to one of Leech's snobs, for
instance ! He tries to hate the haw-haw
swell, and is equally unsuccessful. When
you hate and can draw, you can draw
what you hate down to its minutest details
—better, perhaps, than what you love—so
that whoever runs and reads and looks at
your pictures hates with you.

AN AFFRONT TO THE SERVICE

Omnibus Driver (to Cabby). "Now then, Irish! pull a one side, will you? What are you making at?
Did you never see a Militiar man before!"

[A disguisingly ignorant observation, in the opinion of young Longcliff,
Lieutenant in Her Majesty's Fusilier Guards.—Fun.]—&, March 7, 1867.

SOCIAL PICTORIAL SATIRE

Who ever hated a personage of Keene's beyond that feeble kind of aversion that comes from mere uncongeniality, a slightly offended social taste, or prejudice? One feels a mere indulgent and half-humorous disdain, but no hate. On the other hand, I do not think that we love his personages very much—we stand too much outside his eccentric world for sympathy. From the pencil of this most lovable man, with his unrivalled power of expressing all he saw and thought, I cannot recall many lovable characters of either sex or any age. Here and there a good-natured cabby, a jolly navvy, a simple-minded flautist or bagpiper, or a little street Arab, like the small boy who pointed out the jail doctor to his pal and said, "That's my medical man."

Whereas Leech's pages teem with winning, graceful, lovable types, and

here and there a hateful one to give relief.

But, somehow, one liked the man who drew these strange people, even without knowing him; when you knew him you loved him very much—so much that no room was left in you for envy of his unattainable mastery in his art. For of this there can be no doubt—no greater or more finished master in black and white has devoted his life to the illustration of the manners and humours of his time; and if Leech is even greater than he — and I for one am inclined to think he is — it is not as an artist, but as a student and observer of human nature, as a master of the light, humorous, superficial criticism of life.

Charles Keene died of general atrophy on January 4, 1891. It was inexpressibly

"NOT UP TO HIS BUSINESS"

Cross Bus Driver. "Now why didn't you take that there party?"

Conductor. "Said they wouldn't go."

Cross Bus Driver. "Said THEY wouldn't go? THEY said they wouldn't go? Why, what do you suppose you're put there for? You call that conductin' a bus. Oh! THEY wouldn't go: I like that, &c., &c."—*Punch*, September 1, 1860.

...

...

...

...

...

...and between; his facial features, and
the cloudrid with the haze in the la
wanted a good nose, and he still
more careful and of the eye, more
waiting—all the same were closely
appeared on the mouth...he would be
...time.

...landed her upper arm and across her
Lectins two years, two years before, Canna
Alieta, a common brand name with pan
against the sky... It was a bitterly cold
day, with a need amused for the spareness of

pathetic to see how patiently, how re-signedly, he wasted away; he retained his unalterable sweetness to the last.

His handsome, dark-skinned face, so strongly lined and full of character; his mild and magnificent light-grey eyes, that reminded one of a St. Bernard's; his tall, straight, slender aspect, that reminded one of Don Quixote; his simplicity of speech and character; his love of humour, and the wonderful smile that lit up his face when he heard a good story, and the still more wonderful wink of his left eye when he told one—all these will remain strongly impressed on the minds of those who ever met him.

I attended his funeral as I had attended Leech's twenty-six years before; Canon Ainger, a common friend of us both, per-formed the service. It was a bitterly cold day, which accounted for the sparseness of

the mourners compared to the crowd that
was present on the former occasion ; but
bearing in mind that all those present were
either relations or old friends, all of them
with the strongest and deepest personal
regard for the friend we had lost, the
attendance seemed very large indeed ; and
all of us, I think, in our affectionate re-
membrance of one of the most singularly
sweet-natured, sweet-tempered, and simple-
hearted men that ever lived, forgot for the
time that a very great artist was being
laid to his rest.

And now, in fulfilment of my contract, I
must speak of myself—a difficult and not
very grateful task.   One's self is a person
about whom one knows too much and
too little—about whom we can never hit
a happy medium.   Sometimes one rates
one's self too high, sometimes (but less
frequently) too low, according to the state

GEORGE DU MAURIER

From an unpublished photograph by Fradelle and Young, London.

of our digestion, our spirits, our pocket, or even the weather!

In the present instance I will say all the good of myself I can decently, and leave all the rating to you. It is inevitable, however unfortunate it may be for me, that I should be compared with my two great predecessors, Leech and Keene, whom I have just been comparing to each other.

When John Leech's mantle fell from his shoulders it was found that the garment was ample to clothe the nakedness of more than one successor.

John Tenniel had already, it is true, replaced him for several years as the political cartoonist of *Punch*. How admirably he has always filled that post, then and ever since, and how great his fame is, I need not speak of here. Linley Sambourne and Harry Furniss, so different from each other and from Tenniel, have also, since then, brought their great originality and their unrivalled skill to the political illustrations of *Punch*—Sambourne to the illustration of many other things in it besides, but which do not strictly belong to the present subject.

I am here concerned with the social illustrators alone, and, besides, only with those who have made the sketches of social subjects in *Punch* the principal business of their lives. For very many artists, from Sir John Millais, Sir John Gilbert, Frederick Walker, and Randolph Caldecott downward, have contributed to that fortunate periodical at one time or another, and not a few distinguished amateurs.

Miss Georgina Bowers, Mr. Corbould, and others have continued the fox-hunting tradition, and provided those scenes which have become a necessity to the sporting readers of *Punch*.

To Charles Keene was fairly left that part of the succession that was most to his taste—the treatment of life in the street and the open country, in the shops and parlours of the lower middle class, and the homes of the people.

And to me were allotted the social and domestic dramas, the nursery, the school-room, the dining and drawing rooms, and croquet-lawns of the more or less well-to-do.

I was particularly told not to try to be broadly funny, but to undertake the light and graceful business, like a *jeune premier*. I was, in short, to be the tenor, or rather the tenorino, of that little company for which Mr. Punch beats time with his immortal bâton, and to warble in black and white such melodies as I could evolve from my contemplations of the gentler aspect of

English life, while Keene, with his magnificent, highly trained basso, sang the
comic songs.

We all became specialised, so to speak,
and divided Leech's vast domain among
us.

We kicked a little at first, I remember,
and whenever (to continue the musical
simile) I could get in a comic song, or
what I thought one, or some queer fan-
tastic ditty about impossible birds and
beasts and fishes and what not, I did
not let the opportunity slip ; while
Keene, who had a very fine falsetto
on the top of his chest register, would
now and then warble, pianissimo, some
little ballad of the drawing-room or
nursery.

But gradually we settled into our
respective grooves, and I have grown to
like my little groove very much, narrow

FELINE AMENITIES

"I *wish* you hadn't asked Captain Wareham, Lizzie. Horrid man! I
can't bear him!"

"Dear me, Charlotte—isn't the World big enough for you both?"

"Yes; but your little Dining-room *isn't!*"—*Punch,* February 16, 1884.

though it be — a poor thing, but mine own!

Moreover, certain physical disabilities that I have the misfortune to labour under make it difficult for me to study and sketch the lusty things in the open air and sunshine. My sight, besides being defective in many ways, is so sensitive that I cannot face the common light of day without glasses thickly rimmed with wire gauze, so that sketching out of doors is often to me a difficult and distressing performance. That is also partly why I am not a sportsman and a delineator of sport.

I mention this infirmity not as an excuse for my shortcomings and failures — for them there is no excuse—but as a reason why I have abstained from the treatment of so much that is so popular, delightful, and exhilarating in English country life.

If there had been no Charles Keene (a terrible supposition both for *Punch* and its readers), I should have done my best to illustrate the lower walks and phases of London existence, which attracts me as much as any other. It is just as easy to draw a costermonger or a washer-woman as it is a gentleman or lady—perhaps a little easier—but it is by no means so easy to draw them as Keene did! And to draw a cab or an omnibus after him (though I have sometimes been obliged to do so) is almost tempting Providence!

If there had been no Charles Keene, I might, perhaps, with practice, have become a funny man myself—though I do not suppose that my fun would have ever been of the broadest.

Before I became an artist I was con-sidered particularly good at caricaturing my friends, who always foresaw for me more than one change of profession, and *Punch* as the final goal of my wanderings in search of a career. For it was originally intended that I should be a man of science.

Dr. Williamson, the eminent chemist and professor of chemistry, told me not long ago that he remembers caricatures that I drew, now forty years back, when I was studying under him at the Laboratory of Chemistry at University College, and that he and other grave and reverend professors were hugely tickled by them at the time. Indeed, he remembers nothing else about me, except that I promised to be a very bad chemist.

I was a very bad chemist indeed, but not for long! As soon as I was free to do as I pleased, I threw up test-tubes and crucibles and went back to Paris,

where I was born and brought up, and
studied to become an artist in M. Gléyre's
studio. Then I went to Antwerp, where
there is a famous school of painting, and
where I had no less a person than Mr.
Alma-Tadema as a fellow-student. It was
all delightful, but misfortune befell me,
and I lost the sight of one eye—perhaps
it was the eye with which I used to do
the funny caricatures ; it was a very good
eye, much the better of the two, and the
other has not improved by having to do a
double share of the work.

And then in time I came to England
and drew for *Punch*, thus fulfilling the
early prophecy of my friends and fellow-
students at University College—though
not quite in the sense they anticipated.

I will not attempt a description of my
work—it is so recent and has been so
widely circulated that it should be un-

THE NEW SOCIETY CRAZE.

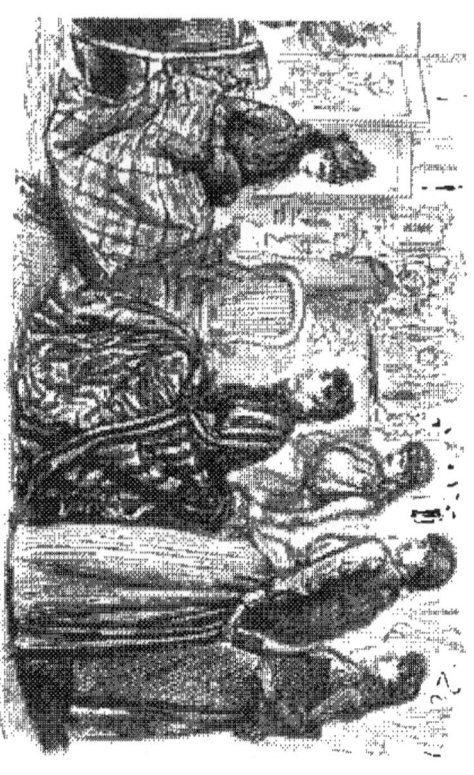

THE NEW GOVERNESS (*showing her pretty teeth*). "Waall—I come right slick away from Ne'york City, an' I ain't had much time for foolin' around in Europe—you bet! So I can't fix up your Gals in the European Languages, no-how!"

HIGHBORN MAMMA (*who learns there's a Duke or two still left in the Matrimonial Market*). "Oh, that's of no consequence. I want my Daughters to acquire the American Accent in all its purity—and the Idioms, and all that. Now I'm sure *you* will do admirably!"—*Punch, December 1, 1888.*

necessary to do so. If you do not remember it, it is that it is not worth remembering; if you do, I can only entreat you to be to my faults a little blind, and to my virtues very kind!

I have always tried as honestly and truthfully as lies in me to serve up to the readers of *Punch* whatever I have culled with the bodily eye, after cooking it a little in the brain. My raw material requires more elaborate working than Leech's. He dealt more in flowers and fruits and roots, if I may express myself so figuratively—from the lordly pineapple and lovely rose, down to the humble daisy and savory radish. *I* deal in vegetables, I suppose. Little that I ever find seems to me fit for the table just as I see it; moreover, by dishing it up raw I should offend many people and make many enemies, and deserve to do so. I cook my green pease, asparagus, French beans, Brussels sprouts, German sauerkraut, and even a truffle now and then, so carefully that you would never recognise them as they were when I first picked them in the social garden. And they do not recognise themselves! Or even each other!

And I do my best to dish them up in good, artistic style. Oh that I could arrange for you a truffle with all that culinary skill that Charles Keene brought to the mere boiling of a carrot or a potato! He is the *cordon bleu* par excellence. The people I meet seem to me more interesting than funny—so interesting that I am well content to draw them as I see them, after just a little arrangement and a very transparent disguise—and without any attempt at caricature. The better-looking they are, the more my pencil loves them, and I feel more inclined to exaggerate in this direction than in any other.

Sam Weller, if you recollect, was fond of "pootiness and wirtue." I *so* agree with him! I adore them both, especially in women and children. I only wish that the wirtue was as easy to draw as the pootiness.

But indeed for me—speaking as an artist, and also, perhaps, a little bit as a man—pootiness is almost a wirtue in itself. I don't think I shall ever weary of trying to depict it, from its dawn in the toddling infant to its decline and setting and long twilight in the beautiful old woman, who has known how to grow old gradually. I like to surround it with chivalrous and stalwart manhood; and it is a standing grievance to me that I have to clothe all this masculine escort in coats and trousers and chimney-pot hats ; worse than all, in the evening dress of the period!—that I cannot surround my divinity with a guard of honour more worthily arrayed!

Thus, of all my little piebald puppets, the one I value the most is my pretty woman. I am as fond of her as Leech was of his; of whom, by-the-way, she is the granddaughter! This is not artistic vanity; it is pure paternal affection, and by no means prevents me from seeing her faults; it only prevents me from seeing them as clearly as you do!

Please be not very severe on her, for her grandmother's sake. Words fail me to express how much I loved her grandmother, who wore a cricket-cap and broke Aunt Sally's nose seven times.

Will my pretty woman ever be all I wish her to be? All she ought to be? I fear not!

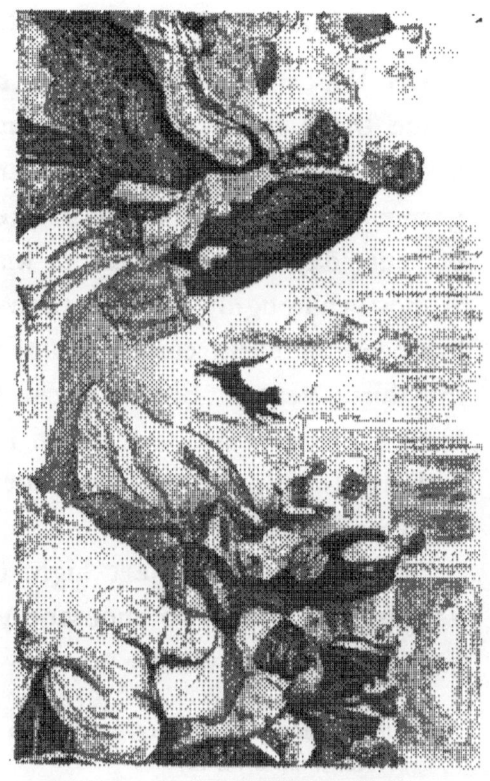

A PICTORIAL PUZZLE.

TENOR WARBLER (*with passionate emphasis on the first word of each line*).—
"He-e-e-ar me once again.
Me-e-e-et me once again."
[*Why does the Cat suddenly jump off the Hearth-rug, rush to the Door, and make frantic Endeavours to get out!—Punch.*

On the mantelpiece in my studio at home there stands a certain lady. She is but lightly clad, and what simple garment she wears is not in the fashion of our day. How well I know her! Almost thoroughly by this time—for she has been the silent companion of my work for thirty years! She has lost both her arms and one of her feet, which I deplore; and also the tip of her nose, but that has been made good!

She is only three feet high, or thereabouts, and quite two thousand years old, or more; but she is ever young—

> " Age cannot wither her, nor custom stale
> Her infinite variety! "—

and a very giantess in beauty. For she is a reduction in plaster of the famous statue at the Louvre.

They call her the Venus of Milo, or

Melos! It is a calumny—a libel. She is no Venus, except in good looks; and if she errs at all, it is on the side of austerity. She is not only pootiness but wirtue incarnate (if one can be incarnate in marble), from the crown of her lovely head to the sole of her remaining foot— a very beautiful foot, though by no means a small one—it has never worn a high-heel shoe!

Like all the best of its kind, and its kind the best, she never sates nor palls, and the more I look at her the more I see to love and worship—and, alas! the more dissatisfied I feel—not indeed with the living beauty, ripe and real, that I see about and around—mere life is such a beauty in itself that no stone ideal can ever hope to match it! But dissatisfied with the means at my command to do the living beauty justice—a little bit of paper,

a steel pen, and a bottle of ink—and, alas!
fingers and an eye less skilled than they
would have been if I had gone straight to
a school of art instead of a laboratory
for chemistry!

And now for social pictorial satire con-
sidered as a fine art.

They who have practised it hitherto,
from Hogarth downward, have not been
many—you can count their names on your
fingers! And the wide popularity they
have won may be due as much to their
scarcity as to the interest we all take in
having the mirror held up to ourselves—
to the malicious pleasure we all feel at
seeing our neighbours held up to gentle
ridicule or well-merited reproof; most of
all, perhaps, to the realistic charm that lies
in all true representation of the social
aspects with which we are most familiar,
ugly as these are often apt to be, with

our chimney-pot hats, and trousers that unfit us, it seems, for serious and elaborate pictorial treatment at the hands of the foremost painters of our own times— except when we sit to them for our portraits; then they have willy-nilly to make the best of us, just as we are!

The plays and novels that succeed the most are those which treat of the life of our own day; not so the costly pictures we hang upon our walls. We do not care to have continually before our eyes . elaborate representations of the life we lead every day and all day long; we like best that which rather takes us out of it— romantic or graceful episodes of another time or clime, when men wore prettier clothes than they do now—well-imagined, well-painted scenes from classic lore— historical subjects—subjects selected from our splendid literature and what not; or,

REFINEMENTS OF MODERN SPEECH

(Scene—*A Drawing-room in "Passionate Brompton."*)

Fair Æsthetic (*suddenly, and in deepest tones to Smith, who has just been introduced to take her in to Dinner*). "Are you Intense?"—*Punch*, June 14, 1879.

if we want modern subjects, we prefer
scenes chosen from a humble sphere,
which is not that of those who can afford
to buy pictures—the toilers of the earth
—the toilers of the sea—pathetic scenes
from the inexhaustible annals of the poor ;
or else, again, landscapes and seascapes—
things that bring a whiff of nature into our
feverish and artificial existence—that are.
in direct contrast to it.

And even with these beautiful things,
how often the charm wears away with
the novelty of possession ! How often
and how soon the lovely picture, like
its frame, becomes just as a piece of
wall-furniture, in which we take a pride,
certainly, and which we should certainly
miss if it were taken away—but which
we grow to look at with the pathetic
indifference of habit—if not, indeed, with
aversion !

Chairs and tables minister to our physical comforts, and we cannot do without them. But pictures have not this practical hold upon us ; the sense to which they appeal is not always on the alert ; yet there they are hanging on the wall, morning, noon, and night, unchanged, unchangeable —the same arrested movement—the same expression · of face—the same seas and trees and moors and forests and rivers and mountains—the very waves are as eternal as the hills !

Music will leave off when it is not wanted—at least it ought to ! The book is shut, the newspaper thrown aside. Not so the beautiful picture ; it is like a perennial nosegay, for ever exhaling its perfume for noses that have long ceased to smell it !

But little pictures in black and white, of little every-day people like ourselves, by some great little artist who knows life well and has the means at his command to express his knowledge in this easy, simple manner, can be taken up and thrown down like the book or newspaper. They are even easier to read and understand. They are within the reach of the meanest capacity, the humblest education, the most slender purse. They come to us weekly, let us say, in cheap periodicals. They are preserved and bound up in volumes, to be taken down and looked at when so disposed. The child grows to love them before he knows how to read ; fifty years hence he will love them still, if only for the pleasure they gave him as a child. He will soon know them by heart, and yet go to them again and again ; and if they are good, he will always find new beauties and added interest as he himself grows in taste and culture; and how much of that taste and culture he will owe to them, who can say ?

Nothing sticks so well in the young mind as a little picture one can hold close to the eyes like a book—not even a song or poem—for in the case of most young people the memory of the eye is better than that of the ear—its power of assimilating more rapid and more keen. And then there is the immense variety, the number !

Our pictorial satirist taking the greatest pains, doing his very best, can produce, say, a hundred of these little pictures in a twelvemonth, while his elder brother of the brush bestows an equal labour and an equal time on one important canvas, which will take another twelvemonth to engrave, perhaps, for the benefit of those fortunate enough to be able to afford the costly engraving of that one priceless work of art,

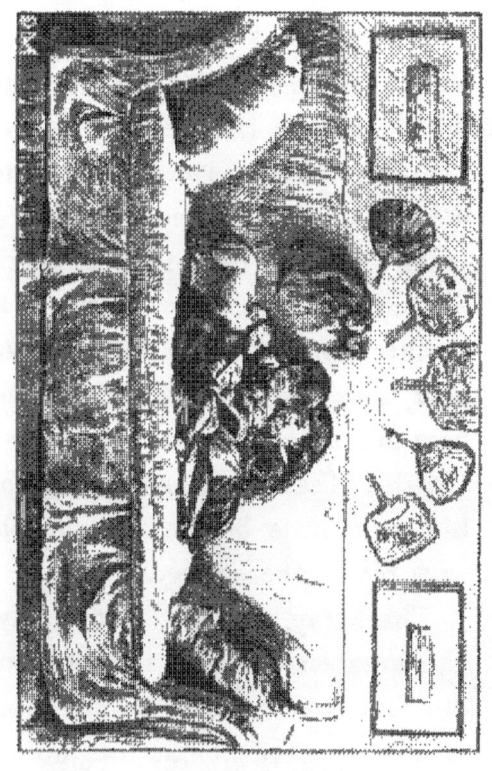

"READING WITHOUT TEARS"

TEACHER. "And what Comes after S, Jack?"
PUPIL. "T!"
TEACHER. "And what Comes after T?"
PUPIL. "For all that we have Received," &c., &c.—*Punch*, February 17, 1866.

which only one millionaire can possess at a time. Happy millionaire! happy painter —just as likely as not to become a millionaire himself! And this elder brother of the brush will be the first to acknowledge his little brother's greatness—if the little brother's work be well done. You should hear how the first painters of our time, here and abroad, express themselves about Charles Keene! They do not speak of him as a little brother, I tell you, but a very big brother indeed.

Thackeray, for me, and many others, the greatest novelist, satirist, humorist of our time, where so many have been great, is said to have at the beginning of his career wished to illustrate the books of others—Charles Dickens's, I believe, for one. Fortunately, perhaps, for us and for him, and perhaps for Dickens, he did not succeed; he lived to write books of his own, and to illustrate them himself; and it is generally admitted that his illustrations, clever as they are, were not up to the mark of his writings.

It was not his natural mode of expression — and I doubt if any amount of training and study would have made it a successful mode: the love of the thing does not necessarily carry the power to do it. That he loved it he has shown us in many ways, and also that he was always practising it. Most of my hearers will remember his beautiful ballad of "The Pen and the Album"—

" I am my master's faithful old gold pen.
  I've served him three long years, and drawn since
    then
  Thousands of funny women and droll men . . ."

Now conceive—it is not an impossible conception—that the marvellous gift of expression that he was to possess in words

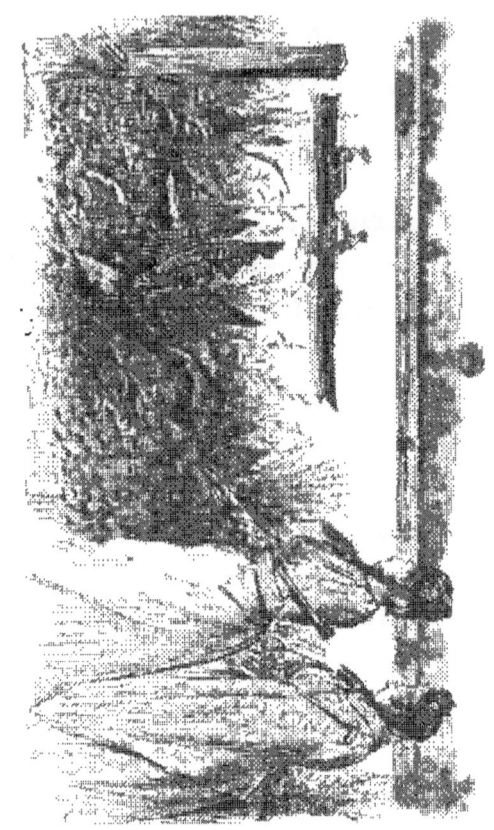

THE HEIGHT OF IMPROPRIETY

Miss GREENMORE, JUNIOR. "There goes Lucy Holfroyd, all alone in a Boat with young Shipson as usual. So impudent of them."

HER ELDER SISTER. "Yes! how shocking if they were Upset and Drowned—without a Chaperon, you know!"—*Punch*, August 8, 1891.

had been changed by some fairy at his birth into an equal gift of expression by means of the pencil, and that he had cultivated the gift as assiduously as he cultivated the other, and finally that he had exercised it as sedulously through life, bestowing on innumerable little pictures in black and white all the wit and wisdom, the wide culture, the deep knowledge of the world and of the human heart, all the satire, the tenderness, the drollery, and last, but not least, that incomparable perfection of style that we find in all or most that he has written—what a pictorial record that would be !

Think of it—a collection of little woodcuts or etchings, with each its appropriate legend—a series of small pictures equal in volume and in value to the whole of Thackeray's literary work! Think of the laughter and the tears from old and young, rich and poor, and from the thousands who have not the intelligence or the culture to appreciate great books, or lack time or inclination to read them.

All there was in the heart and mind of Thackeray, expressed through a medium so simple and direct that even a child could be made to feel it, or a chimney-sweep! For where need we draw the line? We are only pretending.

Now I am quite content with Thackeray as he is—a writer of books, whose loss to literature could not be compensated by any gain to the gentle art of drawing little figures in black and white—" thousands of funny women and droll men." All I wish to point out—in these days when drawing is pressed into the service of daily journalism, and with such success that there will soon be as many journalists with the pencil as with the pen—is this, that the career of the future social pictorial satirist is full of splendid possibilities undreamed-of yet.

It is a kind of hybrid profession still in its infancy—hardly recognised as a profession at all—something halfway between literature and art—yet potentially combining all that is best and most essential in both, and appealing as effectively as either to some of our st ngest needs and most natural instincts.

It has no school as yet; its methods are tentative, and its few masters have been pretty much self-taught. But I think that a method and a school will evolve themselves by degrees—are perhaps evolving themselves already.

The quality of black and white illustrations of modern life is immeasurably higher than it was thirty or forty years ago—its average and artistic quality—and it is getting higher day by day. The number of youths who can draw beautifully is quite appalling ; one would think they had learned to draw before learning to read and write. Why shouldn't they?

Well, all we want, for my little dream to be realised, is that among these precocious wielders of the pencil there should arise here a Dickens, there a Thackeray, there a George Eliot or an Anthony Trollope, who, finding quite early in life that he can draw as easily as other men can spell, that he can express himself, and all that he hears and sees and feels, more easily, more completely, in that way than in any other, will devote himself heart and soul to that form of expression—as I and others have tried to do—but with advantages of nature, circumstances, and education that have been denied to us!

Hogarth seems to have come nearer to

THINGS ONE WOULD WISH TO HAVE EXPRESSED DIFFERENTLY

He. "The fact is I never get any wild fowl shooting—never!"

She. "Oh, then you ought to come down to our Neighbourhood in the Winter. It would just suit you, there are such a lot of Geese about—a-a—I mean *Wild Geese*, of course!"—*Punch*, November 21, 1891.

this ideal pictorial satirist than any of his successors in *Punch* and elsewhere. For he was not merely a light humorist and a genial caricaturist; he dealt also in pathos and terror, in tragic passion and sorrow and crime; he often strikes chords of too deep a tone for the pages of a comic periodical.

But the extent of his productiveness was limited by the method of his production; he was a great painter in oils, and each of his life scenes is an important and elaborate picture, which, moreover, he engraved himself at great cost of time and labour, after the original time and labour spent in painting it. It is by these engravings, far more than by his pictures, that he is so widely known.

It is quite possible to conceive a little sketchy woodcut no larger than a cut in *Punch*, and drawn by a master like Charles Keene, or the German Adolf Menzel,

SOCIAL PICTORIAL SATIRE

giving us all the essence of any picture by Hogarth even more effectively, more agreeably, than any of Hogarth's most finished engravings. And if this had been Hogarth's method of work, instead of some fifty or sixty of those immortal designs we should have had some five or six thousand! Almost a library!

So much for the great pictorial satirist of the future—of the near future, let us hope—that I have been trying to evolve from my inner consciousness. May some of us live to see him!

Printed by BALLANTYNE, HANSON & Co.
London & Edinburgh